This Little Tiger book belongs to:

_____

_____

_____

For JE, MA and SSe, with thanks
— S C

For Haider Bahrani
— T M

LITTLE TIGER PRESS
1 The Coda Centre, 189 Munster Road,
London SW6 6AW
www.littletiger.co.uk

First published in Great Britain 2013
This edition published 2014

Text copyright © Little Tiger Press 2013
Illustrations copyright © Tina Macnaughton 2013
Tina Macnaughton has asserted her right to be
identified as the illustrator of this work under the
Copyright, Designs and Patents Act, 1988

A CIP catalogue record for this book is
available from the British Library

• ISBN 978-1-84895-534-9

Printed in China • LTP/1800/0751/0913

2 4 6 8 10 9 7 5 3 1

I Love You More Each Day!

Suzanne Chiew   Tina Macnaughton

LITTLE TIGER PRESS
London

You're my sunshine, little one,
You are the world to me.

You find such joy and wonder
In everything you see.

I love each happy thing you do,
Each funny thing you say.
From spring to summer, all year through,
I love you more each day.

Each day is bright
and beautiful,
Each day holds
something new . . .

And every day is magical
When it is shared with you.

I love the gifts you give me
And the silly games we play.
Your smiles and giggles warm my heart —
More than words can say.

When summer comes
we splish and splash
In oceans deep and blue.

You show me hidden treasures,
But none so sweet as you.

Each kind and gentle thing you do,
Each thoughtful thing you say,
Makes me so very proud of you.
I love you more each day.

Whether we're
still and quiet,
Watching rainbows
paint the sky . . .

Or whether we're
loud and playful,
Tossing fallen
leaves up high . . .

Each day is an adventure
And filled with so much fun.
New journeys and new friendships
Wait for you, my little one.

You love to stomp
through snowdrifts
As our world turns
sparkly white . . .

And find each pretty, frosted leaf
That twinkles in the light.

Although the seasons turn and change,
Our love will always stay
From springtime through to winter,
I love you more each day.

When sparkling stars shine brightly,
We snuggle up together.
I love you more and more each day,
And more and more for ever!

More heart-warming stories from Little Tiger Press

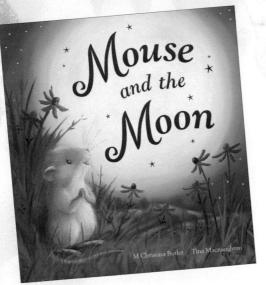

Mouse and the Moon

M Christina Butler • Tina Macnaughton

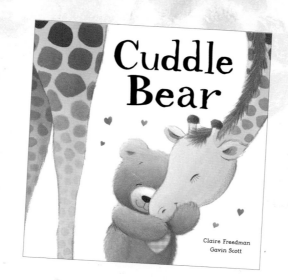

Cuddle Bear

Claire Freedman
Gavin Scott

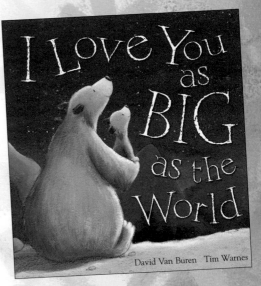

I Love You as BIG as the World

David Van Buren • Tim Warnes

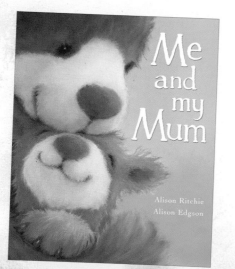

Me and my Mum

Alison Ritchie
Alison Edgson

A sparkly starry book

One Starry Night

M Christina Butler
Tina Macnaughton

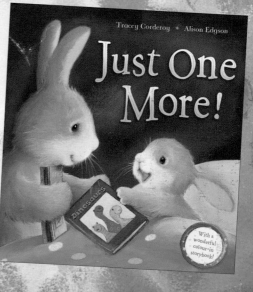

Tracey Corderoy • Alison Edgson

Just One More!

With a wonderful colour-in storybook!

For information regarding any of the above titles or for our catalogue, please contact us:

Little Tiger Press, 1 The Coda Centre, 189 Munster Road, London SW6 6AW

Tel: 020 7385 6333 • Fax: 020 7385 7333 • E-mail: info@littletiger.co.uk • www.littletiger.co.uk